Bilby Moon

Written by Margaret Spurling
Illustrated by Danny Snell

A CRANKY NELL BOOK

Kane/Miller Book Publishers
Brooklyn, New York & La Jolla, California

Dedication

To all those who helped and encouraged me along the way – M. S.

For Louise – D. S.

Danny Snell used acrylic paint on watercolour paper for the illustrations in this book.

First American Edition 2001 by Kane/Miller Book Publishers
Brooklyn, New York & La Jolla, California

Originally published in Australia in 2000 by Working Title Press,
Kent Town, South Australia

Text copyright © Margaret Spurling
Illustrations copyright © Danny Snell

Library of Congress Card Number: 00-109388

Printed and bound in Singapore by Tien Wah Press Pte. Ltd.
1 2 3 4 5 6 7 8 9 10

One night, far away in the desert,

a little bilby left her burrow for the very first time.

She sat still, her ears alert, her nose twitching. She liked the sweet smell of the cool night air, and the soft warmth of the sandy soil. But most of all she liked the moon. It was big and round and shiny and bright, and its silver light was soft and gentle.

Each night when she left her burrow, she looked up to greet the moon. And each night the moon looked down and smiled.

But then one night the moon didn't smile.

Little Bilby was worried.

A piece of the moon was missing!

So that night she searched the ground where the mulga trees grew. She met a hopping mouse, busy looking for seeds and insects.

"Oh, Hopping Mouse," said Little Bilby. "Have you seen the moon tonight? A piece of it is missing!"

"Oh no!" said Hopping Mouse. "I will look in the spinifex grass. If I find it, I will tell you."

Each night, Little Bilby saw that
the moon was becoming smaller.
Sand-dragon was sleeping in a hummock of grass.
He was a wily day-time creature. Perhaps he
would know what was happening.

"Oh, Dragon," said Little Bilby. "Have you seen
the moon tonight? Half of it is missing!"
"Oh dear!" said Dragon sleepily. "I will look tomorrow.
If I find it, I will tell you."

And still, night after night, the moon became smaller and smaller. And the desert became darker and darker. Echidna was scrabbling noisily in the dirt.

"Oh, Echidna," said Little Bilby. "Have you seen the moon tonight? More than half of it has disappeared!"

"That is serious!" said Echidna.

"Perhaps it has fallen into an ant nest. If I find it, I will tell you."

The moon was now just a thin silver crescent.

"I could ask Mole," thought Little Bilby.

"He burrows through the sand. If pieces of the moon
are buried, he might find them."

"Oh, Mole," called Little Bilby loudly. "Have you seen
the moon tonight? Almost all of it has disappeared!"

Mole came up slowly from his sandy world.

"I have never seen the moon," he said sadly. "But I
have heard that it is very beautiful. I will dig carefully.
If I find it, I will tell you."

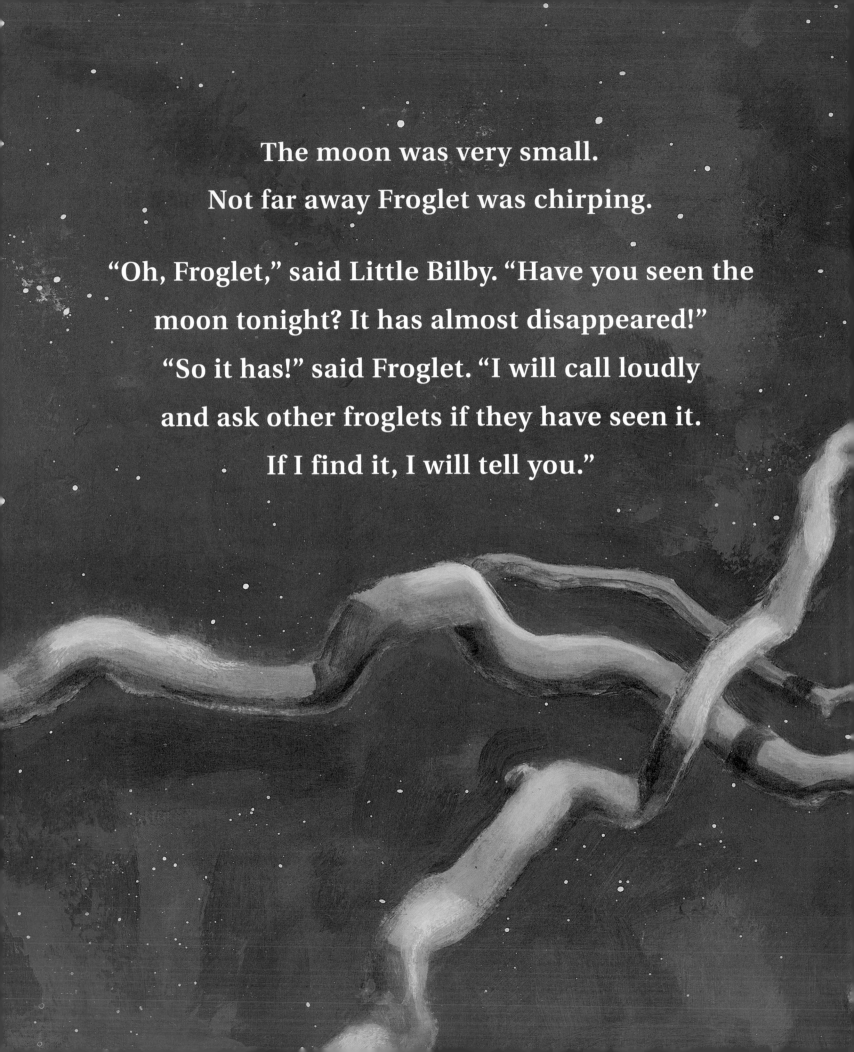

The moon was very small.

Not far away Froglet was chirping.

"Oh, Froglet," said Little Bilby. "Have you seen the moon tonight? It has almost disappeared!"

"So it has!" said Froglet. "I will call loudly and ask other froglets if they have seen it. If I find it, I will tell you."

Then came the night when there was no moon at all.

Little Bilby looked into the vast night sky. Where was
the moon? Strangely, the stars were twinkling more
brightly than she had ever seen before.
But they were not the moon.

Little Bilby felt sad. But she didn't give up.

She searched high. She searched low.

She looked in all sorts of places

where she thought a moon might go.

"What are you looking for, Little Bilby?" came a voice
from the dark. It was Boobook Owl.

"I am looking for the beautiful round moon,"
said Little Bilby. "It has disappeared."

"The moon hasn't really disappeared," said Owl.
"Sometimes we can see it. Sometimes we cannot.
It will come back soon."

And Owl was right, for the very next night a bright silver crescent appeared high in the evening sky.

And each night the moon became bigger and bigger, and the moonlight became brighter and brighter.

Little Bilby hurried off to tell Sand-dragon.
"Have you seen the moon tonight?
Half the moon is back!"

Poor Dragon was confused. First, half the moon
was missing. Now, half the moon was back!
"How strange," he thought, and went back to sleep.

Then one night, as the sky darkened
and one by one the stars appeared,
the beautiful round moon came back.

"Moonlight makes whiskers silver," said Hopping Mouse.

"It sparkles on rocks," said Echidna.

"It glistens on dew," said Froglet.

"I am glad the world has a moon," said Little Bilby.

And they sat on the sand and
told Mole all about the moon.

And the moon smiled.